The future has many faces.

AF201083

In love for Barbara, Alexandra, Kai, Timon, Nele and Isabelle.

Dietmar Dressel

Another day

Stories and tales

To act in love, one has to go an arduous

path.

What drives him and what he always

wants, without really having to do

it, ultimately turns man into

what and how he is.

Dietmar Dressel

Title of the original edition „Tage die das Leben verändern" Copyright © 2012 Dietmar Dressel.

Layout: Alexandra and Barbara Dressel
Printed in Germany

ISBN 9 783751 944465

Content description

The narratives in this book are fictional. The happy and unhappy actions and the deeply sad experiences of the protagonists are a fusion of experiences from the daily life of our time.

The various events are a snapshot that brings people's depth of experience to the limits of their physical and psychological limits. How real life plays in everyday life.

Chapter

Press release by Michel Friedman from April 16, 2012
Lawyer, politician, publicist and television presenter

The author is not a new Goethe, nor is he a Thomas Mann. Fortunately, because that's what makes him so credible.

I cannot say whether Dietmar Dressel speaks to the reader here as an autobiographer or is pure fiction for the best. However, as close as he gets to the reader with his stories, I think that a strong personal connection to the characters must have inspired the author.

The stories are happy, beautiful, thoughtful and deeply sad. Just as life is, a wild roller coaster ride of feelings. Arrival and farewell are central themes of the book. Snapshots that make you happy, invite you to linger and linger long, long.

The book does not educate, it does not teach. Dressel is not an author who wants to show us something. He is not a master of the school but touches him. The book hasn't changed my life, but I may have gained some perspectives. Whatever Dressel got into this book must have been an intense experience. Anyway, I want to read more from this author.

Dressel's work will certainly not be a book of which one will one day say: "What was left of the century". He lacks the provocative of a grass, the ramblings of Thomas Mann, the prepotent of Mario Barth. And there is no magic apprentice in it either. And yet I'm certain that a great author is discovering his talent here.

Bringing a child out of your own belly is as beautiful as a magic piece!

Simone de Beauvoir

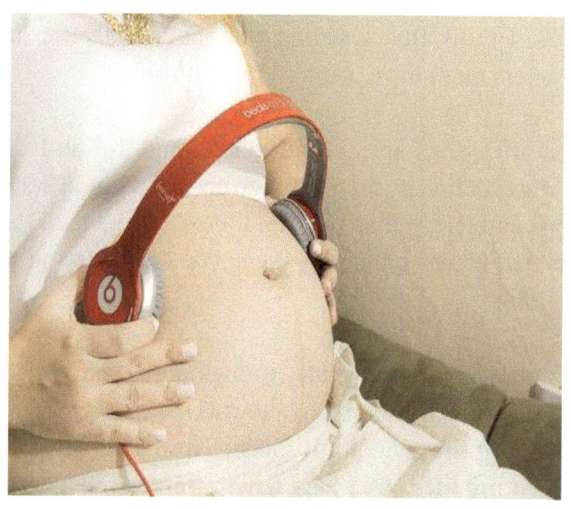

I leave my little world

If the sounds from mom's mouth don't deceive me very much, she sleeps. I think Mama snores with pleasure. Anyway, my dad says if mom should make such strange sounds. I know who my dad and mom are. When they slip into bed in the evening, they sometimes talk about how they supposedly produced me and what fun it was. Especially, my dad said, when they both tried to make my ears. How they practiced this and all of it with pleasure? Well, I do not know. I want to know what was going on there. Maybe it has something to do with mom's bed. As soon as my father slipped into the bed in the evening and the two immediately messed with each other, well I don't know. I have to say that because I can't find any other expression in my head for that.

From time to time Papa said that the appearance of a woman's ears would not be so unimportant, because we women supposedly throw our beautiful head hair back with a sweeping gesture at every opportunity, so that our ears can of course be seen by everyone . For some men, there is even a saying that goes around. I think it starts roughly with the words: "As well as the ears of the woman, so the opening of the body." Actually, this is a bottomless insolence of some men to think of anything, thanks. Thank God I'm in my mother's belly and don't have to bother with the men's world. Maybe I should say -

not yet! Allegedly, at least that's what my mother said when she chatted with her neighbor about God and the world, the Lord in heaven personally created the man out of clay and water. We, we women, were turned out of a rib of this man made by God - thank you! I am really curious to see what will come of me from the created world of men everything.

Ok, of course my dad is an exception and a golden one - of course and I know what I'm saying! Regardless of whether mom is sleeping now, as far as my current location is concerned, I have to admit a kind of cozy warm paddling pool in mom's stomach that I wouldn't have much to say if mom and dad didn't do something every now and then Would bring movement in the immediate vicinity of my living area. Well, movement is meant considerately.

It is pretty uncomfortable for my parents and other people at the moment. It is cold. Thank God it's always nice and warm in my mother's belly. Of course that's important for me! Unthinkable if the water was cold here. The very thought makes me tremble. I don't have much space to move around in my little bathtub. Ok, it's warm, but cramped.

Either I've grown up lately, or mom's tummy can't keep up with my growth. Maybe it all seems so tight to me. Who knows? In any case, better than having to freeze in cold weather.

Mom sometimes talks to Dad about the uncomfortable weather in the winter months and that she should be careful not to fall with me. That would not be so funny for both of us. What is winter? Well, I'll probably find out soon enough.

This brings me to an interesting question that I've been carrying around for some time. I have no idea how to get out of mom's belly? If I have to. And I will have to. I can't spend the whole of my life here in this bathtub. That is definitely not possible. I don't even want to think about how I got into Mom's belly.

Loud ringing noises suddenly distract them from their thoughts. Oh yes, she thinks, startled, the morning alarm sounds are very loud. Mom has to get out of her nice warm bed. Oh sorry. I forgot to say that. My mother's name is Brunhilde. I just want to say that this is her name. Of course I don't call her that. I mentally say mom. I can't speak in Mom's belly.

After the bell with the alarm clock, breakfast is the first thing to do. Of course for both of us. After that it is bedtime. Of course, only for me. Mama will probably drive her car to the supermarket. Shopping! I don't like driving in the car at all. Mom is always so terribly excited. Probably because of the slippery streets and traffic in the city. All of this makes me very restless and anxious. Out of worries about my Mama, I start pedaling wildly and turn somersault after another. In any case, she is not enthusiastic about it.

Finally back in our warm home. Mama is busy unpacking her bags and hopefully will take a little nap after all the cleaning up.

It rings! That too. Hopefully it is not Mrs. Trudberg, our neighbor. She sits and sits with us in the kitchen every time, as if she were chained to the chair. What do I say? As soon as Mama opens the front door, the fat woman's body rolls over through the entrance and runs straight to the chair in the kitchen. As soon as she stands in front of it, she drops heavily on the chair seat and audibly gasps. From the noise of the chair, I can see that this piece of furniture should not be doing particularly well given the weight.

Nothing with the hopedfor slumber hour with my mother. Thank you and no bed. I bet Ms Trudberg's question is about to come up: "How is it, dear little Susan?"

Oh yes, I forgot to say that. My parents chose the name Susan for me. I'm a girl, I know that. Mom and Dad found out from a doctor who was looking for a specific area on my body with a technical device and probably found it. Because since this investigation they call me Susan. To come back to my thoughts on how I got into mom's stomach. So seriously. How did I get in there?

Maybe that has something to do with dad's violent touches in and in mom's body? She is not averse when Papa really gets going. I notice that. On the contrary! Your blood will start to boil and her heart is pounding so hard that I get really scared. What should I do during this time? I'm not asked anyway whether I like it or not.

What if my guess is correct? Well, I don't want to hope that. Here in my bathtub, in mom's belly, it's pretty tight for me alone. Then what if a little Susan, like me, came to me through mom and dad's mess? Well, fear is easing. It really doesn't have to be. Even though? We could then play in pairs.

I want to see the face of my mom if I really get started with the other Susan in our shared bathtub? Well, it was just a thought.

Something pulls me down every now and then. It doesn't hurt. Not really! But it is a strange feeling. And below at all? When I was playing around, I actually didn't notice that there was anything like the bottom of my bathtub.

If I'm drawn to this area, I don't know how to describe it. It makes me scary, yes! At least that's how I feel. Just wanna know what's down there? I feel better in the vicinity of Mama's heart, that is, well up there, and I also have more space there.

And anyway. I have to say that. The powerful movements of Mama's heart take away all fear. Really! It is as if it wanted to tell me with every heartbeat: "I like you very much and protect you! You don't have to be afraid in my stomach." Sometimes so loving and beneficial signals come to me. As if they wanted to tell me how infinitely dear my parents love me and that I am firmly embedded in their hearts.

Wherever I go now, it gets narrower and narrower for me. I will make myself known to mom so that she can see what happens to me. I don't want to go in this direction. Don't you know what I'm supposed to do?

Somehow, mom is busy with other jobs, and every now and then she cries too. I am sure she is in pain. I feel that! Could I be to blame? Maybe that's because I'm so relentlessly pulling me down.

Finally, dad is there. He wants to go straight to the city hospital with mom. That too! I'm definitely not sorry about that. Or yes! I feel good. Except for the painful pulling in the lower part of my bathtub. And mom, as far as I can feel it, nothing is missing. Although she screams violently from time to time and holds on to her stomach. I feel her hand, it is very shaky. Honestly, I no longer understand all of this. Thank God. It doesn't push me down anymore. At least not at the moment. It's strange for a little personality like me. How should a little girl like me know about it? My mom in pain on the way to the hospital. I pulled up and down in my warm bath. This day is not that pleasant either. I just mean.

And again my mom's stomach is getting very tight. If I can express that very considerately. I think mom must have lay down. Whenever she is lying down, at least lately, it gets very tight in my mom's stomach.

For example, striking a balance is no longer possible. It would be better if she got up and decided to take a leisurely stroll. Mom's slight movements are transferred to her stomach and of course to me. This is a pleasant and beneficial rocking every time.

None of the beautiful experiences and the pulling down starts again. Somebody pulls someone unknown to me and wants to push me somewhere without asking if I want it at all and would also like it? As soon as I start to come up with vigorous movements of my arms and legs, mom's stomach presses me down with vigorous movements.

Oh god, mom is screaming again in pain. Hopefully dad is around to get a doctor for help. I'm not particularly well either, and if I could scream, I would. Some wild force pulls me down inexorably. I really can't stop it. Even if I wanted to. And it gets even worse.

Suddenly it gets very cold for me. My cozy warm swimming pool loses its water. That's impossible! I don't know who pulled the plug here. At least not me. Without my nice warm water? How am I supposed to live in mom's belly?

Now my head is squeezed too. It really hurts. I don't want to say more.

I can't move anything anymore. My legs and hands are pressed tightly against my body and the wild pulling doesn't stop either. Do I have to die now maybe? Is that the way I'm drawn to, the way to death?

Please, please dear God, no! That would be terrible. And for my mom too? No, no - please don't! For God's sake, no! Why is she screaming so terribly loud? Dear God - please, please! If either of us has to die, take me! Please take me! How should dad live without mom?

Well! Suddenly everything is gone! I am in no pain. Mom also no longer cries and I can move my head, arms and legs again. I feel really cold for that. If I may say so. All around me is a bright light. It blinds my eyes. Wondering what will happen to me now? My little heart is cramping and my pain is getting worse. I can't take it any longer!

Strong hands hold me on my back and legs. Ouch! Now someone is hitting my butt. So now it's enough! I'm just a little girl. Are you crazy? The fear does not let go and tortures me terribly. Is that the bad hell my dad sometimes spoke of and how scary it should be there?

Suddenly I feel something powerful and lively gathering in my little chest and looking for a way up. I pull my little arms up with all my strength, open my mouth as far as possible and my loud cry for help rushes through the room and seeks its way to my dearest mother - Maaamiii!

The strong hands that hold me gently put me in my mom's arms. I feel a slight thump as I put my little hand on her breast, mom's heartbeat. He gave me all the time in her warm belly the love, confidence and strength to be where I am now.

Papa's lips on my forehead and mom's plump warmth. What an infinitely happy day. I will not forget him in my whole life.

" *I believe that at some point human progress requires us to stop killing our fellow creatures to satisfy our physical desires.*

The size and moral progress of a nation can be measured by how it treats animals. "

Mahatma Gandhi

My domestic pig Hansi

*"Today all races are more or less barbarians towards
animals. It is untrue and grotesque if they
emphasize their supposed high culture at
every opportunity and the most
hideous Cruel millions of
defenseless Commit
creatures or
at least allow indifferent."*

Alexander von Humboldt

A cold November evening, enveloped in an uncomfortable sleet, hangs over Mussbach. A small
village at the foot of the Ore Mountains.

Winter is already coming early this year. Hopefully things
will get better tomorrow, thinks Klaus. He can sleep in
the next day.

I praise my parents' bakery. Thanks to the large oven, it is
always comfortably warm in our house. No matter what
weather we have. Admittedly, in the summer it is sometimes a bit too warm in the house. But better than having
to freeze in the cold.

The school heating system is broken. The caretaker says

and needs to be repaired. The director has arranged a week off for all pupils. The even clip and fold from the bakery wakes Klaus up from his sleep. It is four in the morning. His father puts his first sixty dough blanks in the oven for the round farmhouse breads. With the not particularly tempting thought of having to get up so early every night, Klaus thinks no! I will never learn such a profession. Whether my father likes it or not. With these thoughts, Klaus turns to the other side and continues to sleep.

The tempting smell of fresh bread rolls and the sweet smell of fruit cake and pretzels wake Klaus up from his sleep. After a stopover for a little cat wash in the bathroom, he sits at the breakfast table with his parents. This common breakfast ritual is an integral part of his head.

His mother wipes the toothpaste from his mouth with a small smile and says: „You can make yourself useful today and help me in the kitchen with cleaning. In the shop you have to fill the shelves with the fresh baked goods. You have the next few days off school." „No problem, mom, but first I'll take care of our Hansi, his stomach is sure to growl."

Somehow his parents suddenly seem so depressed when the speech comes to Hansi. Klaus doesn't know that from his parents. Isn't Hansi sick? No, that is hardly possible.

He knew that. Ah, whatever! I'm going to Hansi for the time being, Klaus murmurs to himself. He quickly stuffs the remains of the jam roll into his mouth, wipes his hands on his trousers to the annoyance of his mother and sets off for the stable.

One of his daily duties is to feed Hansi, the family's domestic pig and his friend. His parents gave him Hansi for Christmas. Of course, as a very small piglet. As a big pig that would have been a wrong gift for him. Klaus was allowed to choose the name.

That was perhaps a surprise for him when the little runabout crawled out of the basket and whizzed through the living room, almost ran over the Christmas tree, and could only be caught with great effort by his father.

Thanks to the good care of Klaus and the loving support of his parents, this little Quiekser became a big domestic pig after a few months. In a bakery something always falls off every day. Hansi likes to eat old bread, rolls and cake edges. Boiled potatoes with milk, well stirred and slightly warmed, are undisputed his favorite dishes. He smacks so much that you not only see your appetite, you also hear it.

On the way to his stable, Klaus comes across a heavily built man in a white coat on the farm. Well, he thinks, a strange man in the early morning? What is he doing on our farm? I have never seen it here in the village. He murmurs softly to himself. He hesitantly asks this man and supposed veterinarian, well you could believe him anyway: „Is my Hansi sick?" „No, no! Everything is fine with the sow. And with a smile on his face he says:" „The pig is fine and Hansi is a nice name for your friend." „Yes, it is our domestic pig and a great playmate for me!" „No unnecessary worries! Everything is fine with your Hansi. He has grown well and is also fat."

Hansi trots out of the open stable door towards the courtyard terrace. When he recognizes Klaus, he wants to run towards him, but a man directs him with a stick to the terrace in the direction of the socalled veterinarian. Another stranger, I don't know him either! Well, that is getting more and more beautiful!

The supposed veterinarian approaches Hansi, talks to him quietly, scratches him on the head, on his neck and behind his ears. My friend also seems to like all of this. Klaus mumbles quietly to himself. It annoys him increasingly what the two men do with his Hansi. He stands still and grunts happily to himself. With his other hand, the white coat holds an approximately 20 cm long metal cylinder on Hansi's forehead.

What is that supposed to be, Klaus thinks, and just can't make sense of the whole fuss of these two men. But now it's enough, he thinks angrily. I will immediately ask my father what all this is about? He must know what the two men are doing with my Hansi here on our farm. He turns away from the strange men and Hansi and goes to the front door.

A loud bang, like from a gun, suddenly whips through the air. Klaus stops, startled, turns to the two white coats, and sees Hansi lying on the floor with convulsive twitches. With a knife in hand, one of the two men cuts Hansi's neck. Blood spurts out of the big wound and immediately turns the terrace red.

The sight is unbearable for Klaus. His knees start to tremble, his stomach starts to rebel and dizzy in the head he drags himself with tremendous strength and his whole body trembling in the garden for fear of his friend. Creeps completely out of his mind under a pile of wood and no longer wants to see or hear anything. His stomach can't be calmed down either. He has to throw up.

The fearful screams of his injured soul run through his body and do not want to be calmed down. Just away from this horrible place, he thinks with difficulty. His friend Hansi has to die, how can he go on without him? Darkness envelops him and makes him forget the present. Protectively, it pulls its tormenting thoughts into another world.

When he wakes up, he's lying in his father's arms. His mother, tears in her eyes, holds his hands tight. It's quiet in the room! Klaus feels the warmth and affection of his parents. His physical and mental condition is still weak to talk to his father and mother about Hansi's death. Sleep takes him to another world and lets his thoughts rest.

Like every morning, the scent wakes him up from the bakery. Today it is particularly difficult for him to get up. The experience of yesterday's day weighs heavily on his heart and soul. Everything he had to watch is firmly stored in his head and cannot be suppressed.

Crying crying shakes his body and does not let him come to rest. It is difficult for him to drag himself into the bathroom to soothe his grazing face with warm water. His father unexpectedly comes into the bathroom, takes him in his arms and carries him into the kitchen.

Something doesn't fit with the breakfast ritual today. His mother is already sitting at the table with a tearful face. His father puts him on the corner bench so that he can sit between him and his mother. They look depressed and sad and his father turns to him with a thoughtful face.

„We will never give you an animal again and have it killed for some reason. I promise! My decision to have Hansi slaughtered was not correct! I cannot give you back your dear friend, as much as I would like to do so, Klaus. You have to believe me. Maybe together we can find a way out of this terrible situation. Believe me, it all depresses me and your mother very much." Klaus does not get Hansi back and he feels that he is not alone with his pain. With the promise of his father and mother that he would never again have an animal that belongs to the family killed, his parents relieve him of a heavy burden.

Klaus sits alone at the table for a while. His father is back in the bakery and mother is washing the dishes. He is responsible for drying. It's not necessarily his favorite thing to do, but he does it because it helps his mother at work.

Everything the butcher and his assistant have made of Hansi is given to relatives and friends.

The remaining days pass like in a dream. Klaus is still out of school and he plans to create some order in the garden for the coming winter. Gardening will undoubtedly distract him from his Hansi experiences, and he'll tidy up the stable at the weekend.

Saturday, a day on which his father's bakery is always busy, he will certainly not be able to help him in the stable. Regardless, Klaus thinks, I will look into Hansi's home.

What does the stable look like? Everything full of straw and hay. How does that come here? Isn't there something rustling in there? So I can't use mice here. Let them go to the barn. Funny, in the corner, what is shaking out of the straw, does it look like two long ears? Certainly and guinea pigs are not. I know that much, thinks Klaus. No! A rabbit! And another one besides! Hooray, I have two rabbits!

Two hands lie on his shoulders and hold him. It is his father! „You should go to our neighbors and ask Gottfried's father if he can give you a sack of hay and a small bucket of wheat grains? Thank you for the two rabbits. He gave it to you. Mom gives you carrots and salad." „Yes, Daddy!" „When you're done with your work, you can help me in the bakery!"

Despite the grief for Hansi, he is very happy. The little piglets with his friend Gottfried also help to endure his grief.

It will be a while before the wounds on his soul and heart heal. The two rabbits can of course not replace his dead Hansi, but they will certainly become good friends.

His parents' promise never to kill a pet again will help him overcome the pain of Hansi's death and remain without fear and worry about his two new playmates.

„The thought of the changeability of all earthly things is a source of infinite suffering and a source of infinite comfort.“

Marie von Ebner-Eschenbach

The milk car

Where is the milk car left today, Klaus muses to himself. It should have been here long ago. It is the only large transport car, except his father's small car, which brings a little traffic noise into the village.

Suddenly, engine noises can be heard in the air. Finally, thinks Klaus, the milk car is coming. Our farmers in the village want to get rid of their milk. The cows don't ask if it's Sunday, weekday or public holiday. They want to be milked every day and if the milk should not become a-cidic, it has to be quickly driven to the milk farm in the nearby town.

First squeaky tires of a car, then horribly scary screams tie his feet to the stable floor. You have to help immedia-tely! It pounds in his head. The feet only want to move reluctantly in the direction of the street, as if they already suspected what to expect there.

The milk car is across the street from the entrance to the bakery. The driver of the truck stands at the driver's door, as if stunned, simply unable to move.

On the street, on the big front wheel of the milk car, a small human body. The face is terribly disfigured and full of blood. Despite the bad head injuries, Klaus recognizes his friend Gottfried.

His screams are appalling and his twitching body is a picture of horror. Klaus not only feels it with his heart, but also with every fiber in his body. My God, what can I do to help Gottfried? Thoughts roll over in his head and he cries out for help in need. With effort and great effort, and yet as carefully as possible, he lifts his friend up and drags him to the bakery with his last strength. The warm blood from Gottfried's neck splashed on his face and his friend's hands clenched on his back, beating wildly.

Klaus has to give a terrible picture with Gottfried in his arms. His father quickly runs up to his son, gently takes Gottfried from him and puts him on the baking table. At the same time he calls for his wife to call the emergency medical service immediately - immediately!

A lot of blood flows from Gottfried's right side of the neck, the baking table is immediately colored red. Klaus can no longer absorb all of this mentally. It turns black before his eyes, he slumps and remains curled up motionless on the floor.

The first thing he notices is a white coat and the serious face of a gray-haired older man. This time it's really a doctor. He looks at Klaus seriously with calm eyes, takes his arms in his hands and speaks in a low voice: "You and your parents saved your friend Gottfried's life with your quick help. Without your immediate action, your friend would have bled to death. Gottfried was seriously injured in the car accident. The carotid artery injury has been life threatening. Thank heaven, we were able to stop the bleeding in time. The other serious wounds are very bad, but thank goodness not for your friend.

Even the terrible facial injuries, as terrible as they look, will heal again. A few small scars will probably remain. „I think your friend will be able to go back to school in about three months. You can visit Gottfried with your parents in the hospital next week."

When the doctor says that, his eyes smile. He takes Klaus in his arms and says goodbye.

A cry of joy escapes from his tortured chest and pushes the heavy emotional strain and the terrible event into the background.

Klaus has learned something about life. With his young mind he could understand and feel with his heart that there are days in life that can change everything.

I say this to you in parting: listen to the bird! Listen to the voice that comes from yourself! If she is silent, this voice, know that something is wrong, that something is wrong, that you are on the wrong path. But if he sings and speaks your bird, he will follow him into every temptation and into the most distant and coldest loneliness and into the darkest fate!

Hermann Hesse

A conversation with the inner voice

The connection with the inner self, the being within us, is the only secure foundation, on which you can build your life.

Swami Sivananda Radha

The morning fell into Helmut's bed at six in the morning. Like every day. Bossy and unconditional! Even his name is the same every day - Helmut Fedderson. Always Helmut Fedderson. Not Gustav Fedderson! Wouldn't be that bad either. Does everything in my life have to run like a clock? Not too slow or too fast! Always nice and regular! It's all disgusting, Helmut thinks grumpily.

He doesn't really want that. A portion of variety and sometimes one or two spontaneous actions would do his life good. It is actually more for a relaxed and casual lifestyle. Just want to know who is responsible for this stubborn regularity in my daily life? At least not me, that's for sure.

„Hello Helmut, are you trying to force me on a nonsensical discussion?" What is going on in my head? Or better, who's in my head? Actually, I am awake and with my head, I hope everything is fine. As you know, asking costs nothing, he thinks curiously. „Hello, does someone here want to force me to have a conversation?" „I don't impose anything on you, my dear Helmut, but I will take care of orderly behavior in your life, and that for quite a long time." „Oh no?" „But yes!" „And how do you do it so inconspicuously? Well, at least I haven't noticed anything about your activities. At least not until today!" „Tell me, Helmut, just as an example from many others, you have not yet noticed that you like to be in the morning, especially if the morning doesn't want to show itself from its sunny side at all want to stay in your bed, like today, office or not!" „My God again, it happens! What is so unusual about it?" „What does unusual mean here? Well, you're funny! I, your conscience, you can also say IT to me, if you like that better, I have you in those minutes of doubt that you deliberate on - I get up and go to the office or I prefer to stay in bed for a while - always mentally supported and morally stimulated to fulfill your professional duties in the office." „Oh what? Then did you drive me out of my nice warm bed? That's mean by you!" „It's possible, Helmut, it's possible! But your colleagues are in a way grateful to me for that!"

„So are you commanding my life?" "Admittedly, it's not always easy with you. Ultimately, you're always insightful and follow my advice." "What does advice mean here? You mean your orders!" "I just mean well with you." "Can't you even go on vacation? I don't feel well today. My head is hot like a potato. There is no place in my body that doesn't cause pain. I have don't feel like running to the office just because you think that's right. As my inner voice you should know that! Why don't you even think about my health? You don't have to think about my life-style. I do it myself!"

For a while there is a ghostly silence in his head, as if he had only been dreaming in the past few minutes.

„Yes, Helmut, of course you are right, and the result of my examination is not good for your body." „How do you mean?"

And again his inner voice is silent. Having become restless from the words, Helmut ponders what his inner voice will say.

„You have to go to a hospital immediately!" „That is the last thing I will do! And why? Why should I do that?" „On your last business trip to Senegal, you contracted a dangerous lung disease. The disease is called ARDS. The doctors say: „Acute, progressive lung failure", or shock lung."

You may have inhaled gases at the company where you worked for a period of time that are very harmful to your lungs. The disease is lifethreatening for you. „You must immediately call an emergency medical service. I can't do that for you even if I want to."

„That is getting better and nicer!" „If you can't do that, you will suffocate here in your apartment and I would be rid of my job with you." „Don't you think that for me as a bachelor in the early morning it all a bit much is once?" „Already possible, Helmut. I can't change that even if I wanted to. I can only help you spiritually."

And again the morning comes to Helmut's bed. Today timid and compassionate, so as not to disturb him in the bed. Awakened, Helmut's eyes capture a windowless, mediumsized room. Technical equipment and monitors are installed everywhere on the walls.

His ears hear regular beeps, which cause him to feel restless in a very depressing way. The arms are tied to the left and right of the bed. There is a tube in his mouth through which fresh air is regularly pumped into his lungs and used air is extracted again.

Above him, attached to a pole, is a large bottle with a tube that leads to his left arm and is probably in a vein there.

Something must have happened to my lungs. What did my inner voice say? „Acute, progressive lung failure or shock lung."

Then he comes up with the word breakfast. No wonder, the morning has not yet said goodbye. How is he supposed to have breakfast when the pipe is in his throat? If he pulls it out, he might have to suffocate. If he leaves the tube in his lungs, his stomach won't be thrilled.

A nurse would certainly not be bad in this situation. But how should he organize that? He can't call, the pipe is in his mouth. And he can't do anything with his hands. They are tied to the bed.

Helmut is on the verge of collapsing and his inner voice does not answer to help him in this serious situation. What is the appropriate saying:

„And even if the need is so difficult, a little light comes from somewhere.“

This time in the form of a goodlooking, brunette nurse, which will hardly interest him in his current situation. The main thing is to relieve his pain, which can hardly be endured.

„Good morning, Mr. Fedderson.“ The calm voice pulls him out of his depressed mood. „I'm sister Helga and responsible for her. How do you feel?“ Funny, really very funny! How am I supposed to speak to the pipe in my throat. Well, I'm trying to move my head left and right. She'll understand what I'm saying.

„I understand you!“ Of course, they are not well in this situation. You have been brought to our intensive care unit with a lifethreatening lung disease and need mechanical ventilation. Don't worry, they won't starve. Liquids and medications, especially those for pain relief, are given to them on probes on their left arms. I will suck her lungs every two hours. I will do this very carefully, but pain cannot be avoided entirely. Our chief doctor, Dr. Weber, will speak to you about the further treatment this afternoon. I'm leaving her alone now!

If there is a medically threatening situation with them, I can tell by the beeps. Do not worry unnecessarily and try to sleep."

Sleep? How should I sleep, Helmut thinks grumpily. When he was still healthy in bed at home, and the alarm clock rang early at six, he would have stayed there one time or another. But here in the bedside? No thanks!

If he closes his eyes to sleep, it doesn't last long. If he opens his eyes again, he sees a white blanket and technical equipment on the wall. A window to look out? Are you kidding me? Are you serious when you say that! The room in which it is located must be isolated. He is suffering from a very contagious and dangerous illness.

A male voice interrupts his brooding. „Good afternoon, Mr. Fedderson. My name is dr Weaver. Your emergency call saved their lives. You have contracted a rare lung disease. The mortality rate, i.e. the ratio of deaths to the number of illnesses, is still relatively high, but we are confident that they will get well again."

„Due to advances in supportive therapy in recent decades, the death rate has dropped sharply. Don't worry, they are in the right hands with us. In about twelve weeks they will be home safely."

What a message. He would like to thank the doctor, but with the tube in his throat it is not possible. Crying for joy, he considers how he will reshape his future life.

„Hello, my dear inner voice. Are you still there or have you crumbled out of my body? Helmut mentally calls for his inner voice." „How can you think of me, Helmut?" Answers his inner voice. And with great relief.

„A conscientious and faithful order in persona like me doesn't just disappear so nothing to you just because your body is not doing so well. In any case, I am pleased that you are returning to an orderly life, which I will of course manage and regulate for you." „Oh, dear inner voice. Speaking of regulated life!"

Helmut arranges his world of thoughts and turns back to his inner voice. „Do you know the term ultimate arrangement?" „I know, Helmut! I rarely hear this kind of arrangement, but I know it." „Great!"

„From now on you will keep your mouth shut for the rest of my life, give no more spiritual orders and listen quietly and well as I take my life into my own hands. I will finally be able to do what I want! Did you understand me?" „I hate to do it, Helmut, but I understood it!"

„The whole thing has something good for you too, my dear inner voice. You will learn a lot about real life. Of course you can also leave me and look for another victim. Believe me, it will be exciting and interesting for me. Look forward to the coming time."

It's ghostly, every moment of life wants to tell us something, but we don't want to hear that ghost voice. We are afraid, when we are alone and silent, that something will be whispered in our ears, so we hate the silence and numb ourselves with conviviality.

Friedrich Nietzsche

The only tyrant I recognize in this world is the quiet inner voice.

Mahatma Gandhi

The train of the heart is the voice of fate.

Friedrich Schiller

The Wenceslas Square with its two faces

Days in Prague

Prague, a beautiful city with two faces

All incoming calls should be blocked at night. It would be so comfortably quiet in bed, and dreams remained undisturbed as they wandered through the mysterious world of unexplored spiritual life.

„Hello Pavel, what's so important at this late night hour that makes you ring my doorbell?" „Say Christian, don't you read a newspaper, don't you see any television and don't you listen to the radio?"

„Are you talking about your combative efforts to develop democratic structures in your home country?" „And since I know your attitude on this subject well, I would be happy to meet you here in Prague soon. Of course only as far as your time allows?" „You could have told me that tomorrow morning too." „Excuse me, Christian, my composure has disappeared from my head." „Ok, Pavel, I'm coming." „I I'm happy, Christian! When can you be here?" „I will start my car tomorrow at noon and will be with you in Prague in the late evening."

The night at Pavel is not for sleeping. The discussions don't want to end. A small breakfast in the morning and sleepy as everyone is, it goes to the protest rally on Prague's Wenceslas Square.

What follows after an hour of peaceful protests by the demonstrators can only be compared to a terrible nightmare. Christian didn't even get a slap in the face from his parents, or a spanking.

Armored personnel carriers, water cannons and a large number of personnel carriers with armed police officers drive with no regard for the traffic, purposefully to the place where thousands of demonstrators have already gathered. Thugs of the police and soldiers of the army brutally attack the peaceful protest march.

Christian is almost passed out from the blows of the soldiers. Together with other demonstrators, they are thrown onto a vehicle.

After a short drive, the police vehicle brakes and stops. Christian cannot see anything, a sack over his head prevents that. A gate is opened. The police vehicle drives into a courtyard and stops again. With loud shouting, of course in the Czech language, the wounded demante is ordered to climb off the police car immediately. A real roar if it weren't that serious.

Since Christian doesn't understand the shouting, he stays there. A policeman pulls him from the police car and drops him on the floor. Another policeman pulls the hood off his head, grabs him by his jacket and drags him like a piece of wood into a windowless room. There he throws him on a wooden bench and locks the door.

Some time later, the same policeman comes and beats Christian, who can only move with great pain, like a piece with powerful blows and kicks in a dirty room.

Regardless of his injuries, he pulls things off his body and sprinkles him with a cold jet of water for minutes.

After this torture tour, he throws a bundle of clothes on the wet floor and, with a loud roar, makes it clear to him to put the clothes on.

Christian lies on the cell floor with a blanket in his hand and is exhausted seconds later and at the end of his strength in another world.

It is late at night. A weak lamp lights up matt on the low

cell ceiling and bathes the room in a diffuse light. Christian is slowly finding his way back to reality. He sees men running around the cell like dark shadows. Two of them are sitting on his mattress and are carefully trying to clean his face injuries from the blood with a rag. These efforts, as well as they are meant, cause additional pain and make him fully awake.

The events of the past few hours are violently falling into his consciousness. Police officers' batons, boots, and fists have made one big wound out of his face and body.

The face is swollen. Christian sees everything through a fog. His pain is unbearable. It is difficult for him to say which part of his body is not affected. In his brittle voice, he thanks the few words he can speak in Czech and introduces himself to his helpers. The two do the same.

„My name is Michael and I'm a doctor." The older of the two introduces himself. „Your condition is catastrophic. Anyway, that's my first impression of you. I cannot assess possible internal injuries. I would have to examine you more closely. What is impossible in this prison cell."

„Your life is not immediately threatened, but you must be examined urgently by a doctor. What brutal brawl did you get into?" „Yes, it's true! Me and many other peaceful demonstrators have been brutally beaten, but for different reasons than you might think."

And Christian begins to tell his experiences on Wenzels-platz in Prague. There is an unusual silence in the room. You hardly hear the prisoners' breath. Some wipe their eyes with their sleeves. Nobody speaks a word.

Suddenly loud closing noises. The cell door is opened and two prison guards, each with a baton in hand, storm in like wild buffaloes, scream and roar around and brutally beat all the prisoners until each of them lies on his mattress with both hands over his head .

The policemen are proud of their actions, laugh and pat themselves on the back with approval. When the two police officers leave the cell, one of them kicks Christian in the back with his boot. His cries of pain probably sound like music to these cops.

The cell door is closed and with their keys they clatter on the cell doors for a while.

And again the prisoners are looking for a place in this small, dark prison cell for rest. It is the fear of violence and humiliation that makes her cry. The saving sleep brings peace to everyone for a few hours.

Another rattle of keys on the cell doors. It's supposed to be the morning alarm clock. Pain-distorted by the nightly beating by the police, Christian's inmates try to arrange their mattresses. Michael gently reaches under Christian's arms and raises him up. „Christian, your condition is terrible!" „Michael, I have to go to the bathroom urgently." „We don't have a toilet here in the cell!" „Do I have to call these police officers?"

Michael takes Christian's arm and leads him into the corner next to the tiny grid hole in the outer wall. There Christian discovers a covered metal bucket. Now he also realizes where the terrible and unbearable stench of feces in the cell comes from. No matter how he breathes, with nose or mouth, he has to vomit.

He looks incredulously at Michael, who has discreetly moved away from him, and then looks at the bucket in the corner. „No Michael! I can't! Really not! We're not in the Middle Ages!" „But yes, Christian! This applies particularly to political prisoners. In the eyes of the government of our country, we are traitors, enemies of the state and collaborators!"

The FRG buys political prisoners from the prison GDR. You don't have to suffer long in a prison. "What did we do to be treated like this Michael?" „What are those politicians who govern so inhumane?"

„Don't look at me like that, Christian! In front of you is a hero with his cellmates who want to change that and where are we? In a prison in Prague. Everyone you see here in this cell dreams and fights for political change in our country." What a human tragedy, Christian thinks quietly. And he sees the events of the Prague Spring in front of his eyes like in a documentary. The last thoughts he's deliberately trying to work on in his head are more than daunting.

There is also a light in these bad prospects. Christian thinks vigorously about what's to come. Interrogate, convict, prison! With a little luck, expulsion to the FRG.

Christian is aware that the days in Prague will fundamentally change his attitude towards the politics of socialist states and his future life.

He has to vomit and loses consciousness. A consolation for him not having to think about what will come in the next few days. Experiences that he will certainly not soon forget.

No one would come up with the idea today that the Tibetan monks had no idea about economic liberalism and their rebellion against the Chinese occupation was pointless because a totalitarian or authoritarian system could not be improved.

If you do not have freedom, you certainly cannot go headless to achieve it, but you cannot afford armchair wisdom. So the Prague reformers and those who wanted to go further certainly made a number of mistakes; but for their defeat on August 21, the global political constellation and Moscow's claim to power were decisive. In the first months of 1968 a strong breeze blew through the country, which encouraged people. Two years later, after allowing half a million people to flee west, the country was "normalized" for almost two decades. The borders became tight and the people were silenced.

The New Zurich Times

If everything seems to be going against you, remember that
an airplane takes off against the wind,
and not with him.

A popular saying

An uncertain flight

*Since there have been border guards, barbed wire fences
and minefields, people have been able to fly.*

Dietmar Dressel

What a nice and lukewarm September evening in downtown Leipzig. It would be better if we met in the penguin bar, Joachim thinks, and continues to stroll towards the Erdener podium. A discreetly furnished restaurant in the middle of the old town of Leipzig and with excellent cuisine.

During the Leipzig Autumn and Spring Fair, it is not so easy to get a seat in this popular place. Hopefully Petra has already reserved two places, otherwise it will be difficult to discuss an escape plan while standing and with an empty stomach. My stomach would be happy if he got something tasty to eat. He's been growling since noon anyway. Joachim mumbles to himself and opens the door to the restaurant.

„Hello Petra, nice that we can both sit and eat in peace. How was it in the office?" Joachim's fiancee is the section head at the German University of Physical Education in Leipzig and is responsible for the competitive swimming area.

„My team is in Rome for a swimming competition! I can't be there because of my relatives in West Germany. My office is swept clean and I have more time for myself and of course for you too."

„I would like to introduce our trade fair guest, Mr. Reinhold from Düsseldorf. You know, my mother always rents to West German fair guests during the spring fair and autumn fair."

„Good evening, Mr. Reinhold, how do you like our beautiful Leipzig and how satisfied are you with the trade fair offer and your trade fair business?" „I don't want to judge this city negatively. There is still a lot of sights to be improved. But I feel very well accommodated by her friend's parents. Business with my trade fair partners from Poland is going well."

One can see from his facial expression that he does not want to go into this subject in more detail and Mr. Reinhold also changes the subject. „From the conversations with Petra's parents, especially with her father, did I learn about her planned vacation trip to Bulgaria. Why this country of all places? What do you like so much there? Are you not interested in spending your vacation in Spain, Italy or France?" „Please be a little quieter, Mr. Reinhold!" „Oh, sorry! Every now and then I forget that I'm in the GDR."

„We like to go to Spain, Mr. Reinhold, but that is too expensive for us, even if we both earn very well. We currently have a conversion factor between the GDR brand and the FRG brand of six to one. To exchange a Westmark" We have to pay six GDR marks. Assuming that a threeweek vacation trip to Spain costs us about three thousand West Marks, then this corresponds to about Eighteen thousand Marks of the GDR. We can buy a car for that.

„For a trip to Spain, i.e. Western Europe, we need permission from the authorities in the GDR. It will be difficult. Formulated carefully." „I understand that! But again on the subject of holidays in Western European countries.

And Mr. Reinhold speaks a little quieter. „Klaus Rüdiger, a tennis partner in our club, told me two weeks ago that his nephew from Erfurt in the GDR spent his vacation in France with the authorities in the GDR without any problems."

Mr. Rheinhold interrupts Joachim's enticing thoughts of sun, beach and sea and continues with his explanations. „He is said to be a doctor in a hospital in Erfurt. So do not belong to a special party class." „Oh no! It is not by chance that a duck from a West German tabloid, Mr. Reinhold?" „No, Joachim! Klaus Rüdiger doesn't tell me any girls! "

„Once assumed, that's all true. Ultimately, the question remains, how did he organize it? Or, who approved it here in the GDR? And why exactly a doctor from Erfurt? Does the person have special privileges? Does he only medically treat high Stasi officials or members of our government? "Joachim asks a little incredulously. You can see the doubts on his face. „Yes, how did he organize it?" Mr. Reinhold speaks softly. „As far as I can remember the conversation, there should be a regular scheduled flight of the GDR Interflug Gesellschaft from Dresden to Prague. There he waited for a Lufthansa aircraft that flies daily from Munich via Prague and Budapest to Istanbul. The time interval between the two planes, i.e. arrival of the GDR plane and onward flight with the Lufthansa plane, were only about thirty minutes. So no more than a little coffee break. He probably stayed in the transit area of the Prague airport during this time, and of course saved himself all the customs controls at the Prague airport."

„He hid in the toilet in the meantime, probably in order not to arouse unnecessary attention from the airport police. I don't know how he organized the approval for the onward flight with the Lufthansa aircraft to Istanbul. In Istanbul he reported to the German Embassy and two days later he was in Düsseldorf. And to go on vacation from there is no problem." „Oh! And where's the doctor now?" „In Düsseldorf!" „Oh no! It's like a hit in the lottery!" Breathes Joachim completely amazed!

„I have to apologize to both of you. I'm still meeting with a business friend from Poland and have to leave her alone! "" I'll see her tomorrow with her parents. Or do you want to skip breakfast?" „No, Mr. Reinhold, I'm looking forward to it."

Mr. Reinhold says goodbye to them and rushes to his business meeting. „Petra, I pay our bill and discuss everything else in the park. There are too many people here and some of them have big ears."

They look for a bench in the parking lot, snuggle up like a couple in love and enjoy the pleasant evening air.

„Once assumed, Mr. Reinhold does not lie to us. The risk we have to take is comparatively small. What have we thought about in order to come to Western Europe forever and escape from the GDR. In no case do we risk our lives if we flee with the Lufthansa aircraft. We will not organize a shootout in the airport building, but behave inconspicuously like all other passengers."

Where's the risk for us, Petra? What do you think? „Joachim, are you sure that all of this is not just a wild story?" „Ok, possible? It would be worth trying. We cannot be shot, we cannot drown, and there are no mine fields in an airport building."

If we find on arrival in Prague that the flight of the Luft-hansa aircraft via Budapest to Istanbul does not exist thirty minutes later, we take a walk in Prague and fly back home.

I will also book the return flight. As a precautionary mea-sure, so that no one in the travel agency could think wrong. We both run the risk of being arrested and detai-ned at the airport. Yes, we have the risk! It is small, but it is possible. Ok, then we make an application in prison to withdraw GDR citizenship and leave for the FRG.

If we are lucky we will be bought by the FRG from the GDR prison misery and deported to the FRG. It may take a year or two, but we don't risk our lives under any cir-cumstances. The GDR lacks foreign exchange, i.e. DM, dollars and other western means of payment. The ninety thousand Westmarks that they receive from the FRG for every political prisoner is a welcome gift.

„Do we want to risk it? What do you think, Patra?" „Ok, Joachim, it might not be wise of us not to follow fate!" „Ok, Petra, what is the saying so aptly":

„What you can get today, do not postpone until tomor-row."

„I will take care of the plane tickets to Prague this week. We tell your and my parents that we want to spend a weekend in Prague. Don't forget to pack all our documents, we need them in Munich!"

With a pounding heart, Joachim stands at the travel agency near Karl-Marx-Platz and thinks very carefully about what questions the employees might be asking him. Half an hour later, he is holding two plane tickets to Prague. Departure next Saturday. Booked and paid for return flight. He cannot believe that all of this was possible without complications. Whenever something seems easy, Joachim thinks, you have to think very carefully. There is also a saying:

„The better part of bravery is caution.“

The last day before the big event arrives faster than expected. Tomorrow both want to go a way that one cannot take without risk from the GDR to West Germany.

Many lose their lives, take great damage to their health or involuntarily march to prison. Actually absurd considering that there are people who, for whatever reason, only want to live in another country. If it weren't all that serious, you might think it could only be a political joke.

Joachim and Petra sit in their favorite restaurant and discuss their escape plan at the table. A beer for Joachim and a glass of red wine for Petra are a must to relax the body and possibly the mind.

„Dear Joachim, I am very excited. What is our timetable for tomorrow?" „The train from Leipzig to Dresden leaves at tenfifteen. We are in Dresden at twelvetwenty. A taxi takes about thirty minutes to the airport. The plane to Prague departs at three forty. The time cushion should be sufficient to compensate for unplanned delays on the train journey to Dresden."

„Joachim, everything is going so well, I'm really getting restless" „Who do you say that to? The thoughts are mine." Never mind. Dear Petra, leave no message to your parents tomorrow when you say goodbye. The time until we can possibly see each other again can be long. Tell your parents, we spend two days in Prague, go shopping and on Sunday evening in the Prague Opera. Monday we are back home in Leipzig. I tell my parents the same.

The time has come, Petra and Joachim take the Interflug plane to Prague on time. The loud engine noise of the Russian machine is a loud obstacle for every chat. Whatever it is, the short distance from Dresden to Prague is quickly overcome and the exhausting noise of the motorbike has to be endured by both, together with the other passengers.

„What we need now, Petra, are good nerves, a handful of courage, a lot of patience and good luck. And as much luck as possible."

The Russian Ilyushin eighteen aircraft slowly rolls to its stand on the airport grounds. A bus takes all passengers to a building at Prague Airport.

„Ok, what now, Joachim?" „I'm going to ask a customs officer where the toilets are, we got sick from flying." „Ok, do it! It's not that wrong. I'm really sick, but not from flying!"

After a few minutes Joachim goes to Petra, takes her by the arm and walks with her to two doors, which are clearly marked as a toilet. „So, Petra, quickly put on other things and don't forget to put on your wig. Make sure that nobody is watching you in the toilet! We have to do without our suitcases, we don't have time for that. It is too risky. The plane from Munich has already landed. It's on the scoreboard. The story is true for now."

„Now comes the most dangerous stage." „Tell us, could we not just skip this section?" „Well, you still have a sense of humor. Ok, Petra, watch out! We meet in ten minutes in front of the toilet door, then go inconspicuously to the exit and join the other passengers on the way to the Lufthansa aircraft in Budapest." „Ok, Joachim, I hurry!"

Minutes later, they are both standing in front of a flight attendant on the Lufthansa aircraft. "Your tickets please!" The friendly voice of the stuart travels Petra and Joachim out of their thoughts. Crippling fear finds a place in her brain and slowly crawls into the legs, which suddenly don't want to stand on the floor so safely anymore. „I can't take it any longer!" Petra breathes quietly to Joachim! Both are about to decide whether to fly or they are transferred to the airport authority as socalled blind passengers.

„Your tickets please!" Oh, yes, thinks the Stuart. His voice has become a little more impatient. „Please have a moment. I can't find the tickets." „He says as calmly as possible and looks around in his travel bag." „Please stop in the anteroom, I'll be right back!"

Two minutes later, the Stuart appears with the captain of the plane. He looks at them briefly. „How do you get on board our machine?" The voice doesn't sound unfriendly, but that doesn't say much, Joachim thinks. He gathers up all his courage and explains the question of: How did you get on the Lufthansa aircraft?

For some time there was silence and Joachim and Petra reached the limit of their resilience. Both know with their alert minds and with their hearts they feel that the next words of the captain will change their common life decisively without being able to influence them.

The captain looks at her and then points to the flight attendant. "The Stuart will show them their places. You pay for the flight tickets when you are in Munich at one of the

Lufthansa offices there! And they want to go to Munich. With a sympathetic smile, the captain says goodbye and heads for the cockpit.

Joachim's scream echoes through the plane. A scream that expresses the agony of the past few hours and the endless joys. Petra puts her face on Joachim's chest. She is infinitely happy to be able to start a new life together in a free world with Joachim.

The airplane doors close quietly and the machine heads for Budapest to Istandbul into the free world.

When parents die, the past dies. When children die, the future dies.

Dietmar Dressel

Love and pain

With the window wide open, a man with light gray middleaged head hair sits at the desk and tries to do two things at the same time easily and calmly. The abundance of daily business mail, which is still looking for a free space on his desk and the nature awakened from hibernation, the mild breath of spring of which makes its way through the open window and tries to distract him from his work.

It is difficult for him to evade this mysterious magic. Unfortunately, his day-to-day work and the daily rhythm are determined by the work discussions with his employees, telephone calls and meetings.

It is inconceivable that the usual workflow would stop once and without any transition. A private phone call this late morning doesn't fit into the usual office atmosphere at all. The patient, his daughter Dorothea is meant, was critically injured in the head in a traffic accident. Her condition is in a very critical condition. His immediate coming is urgently needed.

Immobile and petrified, he is now sitting in his office chair, unable to move or perceive his surroundings. This message is slowly and painstakingly looking for a way to be heard and the mind refuses to accept the ominous words. With all his might, his mind defends himself against this message. His heart contracts convulsively and the hands helplessly seek a hold. It is difficult for him to organize his thoughts. The eyes, clouded with tears, are desperately seeking God's help.

Slowly his mind tries to perceive this news and in his head the panic tries to win with violent violence.

In these minutes, unable to take any action, he asks a colleague to drive him to his daughter's hospital. The secretary please call his wife so that she can get home as soon as possible.

Now he is stunned at the bedside of his daughter and sees her the way he never wanted to experience it. It is like looking into a dark abyss, on the bottom of which only infinite suffering and pain are waiting.

The father's thoughts circle around this fateful crater like wild eddies. Can his daughter be saved from falling out of their life together? Or will it be taken from them forever?

Crying and writhing in cramps, he tries not to finish thinking the terrible thoughts. His heart screams desperately in pain and rears up against the burden that he no longer wants to carry and still cannot defend himself against it.

The father thinks he can hear a voice. It is not true! No,

no - for God's sake no! It's just a terrible dream. And to God he desperately calls: Take me, take me, but save our daughter!

An inner voice, as if awakened by a ghost hand, whispers softly to him: If you don't feel her breath, you don't feel her heartbeat and the warmth of her skin. The little laborious sighs that escape from her tortured chest? She lives! Don't you feel her struggle with death, which she wants to defeat with all her strength. She doesn't want to lose you and be unwanted to be alone in another world without her parents and siblings.

Of course, she also doesn't want to have to lose life on earth, which she can't end at such a young age. She has only had this life once.

The door to the hospital room opens slowly and a soft, brittle voice murmurs: "Good afternoon!" There he stands, the one who knows more, but you can't see that on the doctor's face. The father's eyes suck on the man's face in the white coat. What will his mouth say Will his words destroy all hopes or give the day strength and confidence?

„You have to make a decision!" These words sound dark and incomprehensible to the father, and remain in the room like ghostly scraps of fog.

The doctor continues to speak quietly. „Her daughter's brain was irreparably damaged by the serious head injury caused by the accident. Important functions such as breathing and cardiac activity can only be maintained through our immediately initiated lifesustaining medical measures. There is nothing more we can do for her daughter! There are limits to our medical options for this severe brain injury."

Her daughter's organs, unlike head injuries, have remained intact and could be very helpful to other seriously ill people, and possibly prolong their lives for a limited time.

The doctor speaks the last words carefully and in a low voice. Difficult to grasp such thoughts at all, the father asks the doctor in his soul pain: „Is there no hope for our daughter? Can't save her life? Are the medical options at the end? Then what decision should I wrest from death?"

The doctor's words come from a strange room. „It is an aid for very sick people. With the organs of their daughter, they give them hope that they may be cured of their illness so that they can still live for a limited time."

Completely desperate, the father wonders, and turns to the doctor for help. „Is our daughter dead now or isn't she? And what do you really mean by your question?"

„How is it possible that our daughter's organs can help other people? Or is our daughter not really dead?" „The doctor turns to the father and only shakes his head." „Your questions are not so easy to answer quickly. I have already said that the severity of her daughter's injury limits the medical and medical options."

What should I think of such words in my current situation? How should I make a decision if I don't get answers to my questions? Now the father thinks in horror. Isn't our daughter's living body a sack full of healthy and usable organs? Or does the doctor only see our daughter like this? Then what is life and what is death?

Despite the damage to her brain, our daughter's living body is a highly complex system that still maintains many subsystems. I feel the warmth of her body and her struggle with the death she wants to defeat.

With all his strength, he feels his daughter's thoughts and her painful and fearful cries for help.

Why do you want my body? I want to live! I want to live, dad! I want to be with you! Don't let me go to another world alone!

With these thoughts, it is very difficult for the father not to lose his mind. Why shouldn't our daughter stay alive just because one should help the body medically for a certain time to heal the serious injury? What do we know about our brain and its ability to organize itself. We just have to give such recovery processes the time, patience, and help. Does only and without exception count the sick person who needs an organ and not the sick person who wants to and could get well again if one took care of him?

Should we give hope to another person with our daughter's organs if we have to banish our daughter to another world in which she does not want and in which we cannot follow her? Does only the suffering person who needs an organ have the right to life? Does our daughter have to die for another person to live? Although she is actually not dead and could live too?

How insensitive you have to be the parents, especially in such a terrible situation, in which the daughter is fighting for her life to ask if they want to allow the organs that their child's hope for life is taken away?

What kind of pathological morality would that be? And where is the respect for human life and dignity? No matter whose life it is.

Both seriously ill people have a right to life! In this situation, which is very difficult for us to bear, how can you ask us whether we want to donate our daughter's organs? Dorothea is not a purpose or a thing for us parents! She is our daughter we love and don't want to lose!

It is unbearable for us to see how she is lying on the bed and suffering and fighting for her life. Should we also allow someone to cut out her organs while she is alive and then hand over the rest of the rest to us for burial?

For us parents, with such a decision, all hope of saving our daughter is lost, irretrievably lost! Or how should we understand all of this? If we can understand it at all in our situation. That is completely abnormal! With these thoughts the father has to think of a quote from N. Ostrowski:

„The greatest good that man has is life, it is only given to him once."

Whose life is the doctor actually about? The father now questions himself in despair. If life is to be the greatest good for all people, organ donation, and the doctor certainly believes this, could be a helpful way to keep a sick person alive for a limited time. But why should we donate our daughter's organs if she is still alive and could possibly be saved if one would make an effort.

And if everyone's life is so irreplaceable, why do we allow many children on our earth to starve to death in agony and suffering during the same time that an organ transplant is to be performed? For God's sake, why? These children also have a suffering organ, their stomach. Who screams in pain, but not because he is sick, but because he only needs something to eat to get well again. Is life as the highest good only intended for a certain class of people? Do children and very seriously injured people, of whom one only really needs their organs, belong in another class? And are they less livable?

Are we children so indifferent with their pleading looks, their already aged face, which can no longer absorb the unspeakable suffering and fear of starvation? Are we ready to divide life into worth living and not worth living? Do we divide death into dead and not really dead? Are we then one thing when death occurs and if we are not completely dead a body whose organs should only serve one purpose?

Do we really want that? Or, when the time has come, do we let people go to another world in peace and without harming their soul?

Kneeling at his child's sick bed, the father is at the end of his strength. Now, in the hour of his most severe mental hardship, he should make a decision that her organs should be removed alive.

It is terribly bad for his daughter to be forcibly deprived of her young life, to be unable to start a family and to live a happy life. He doesn't let his daughter's soul get damaged either!

His self-consciousness answers in a low voice: "What use would a person be if he won the whole world and lose himself or take damage to his soul."

The father's answer is quiet but firm. "No! "We parents won't let our daughter be killed!"

A longing cry makes its way through the vastness of the universe and looks for the parents, siblings and friends who have to stay on earth for a while.

"Do not speak of my departure full of grief, but close your eyes and you will see me among you, now and always. "

Khalil Gibran

When you say goodbye there is a moment when you feel the grief so strongly that the loved one already is no longer with you.

Arthur Schopenhauer

You who have loved me so do not look at the life that I have ended, but at the life that I am beginning.

Aurelius Augustinus

But I feel your calls and your pain when I rest in me as lifeless. What pain in this miserable life is greater than the unfulfilled longing that cries and does not want to rest.

Dietmar Dressel

The Grief is like death

The thoughts that you are looking for, your soul that calls for her and your heart that longs for her so much do not let your parents rest. It has become lonely and quiet near her. The silence of the grave pervades its surroundings like a neverending terrible nightmare. Everything in her house calls for the daughter. Her child's room feels abandoned and sick with a longing for her carefree laugh, for happiness and joy in life.

Everywhere in the places she loved, they are looking for her and yet find only loneliness and infinite emptiness. Where are you? Where can we find you The parents always think. And the cries for help from the daughter after the father, mother and sister rush through the boundlessness of the universe like an echo. The calls try to suppress the feeling of loneliness and emptiness, in vain!

Unintentionally and violently, the daughter is sent to another world and can no longer reach her parents. How should she find her way in loneliness and in the vastness? How should she feel the warmth, love and security of her parents again, which she longs for so much? Where are the hours, days, years when their path together was still connected to their hearts?

Paralyzed, numb, and dazed, the thoughts of the father, mother, and sister move in search of an answer. Everything is so unreal and without a stop. The soul writhes in grief and pain and does not want to be appeased. She reares up and tries to find the daughter with her cries for help. All of these efforts are in vain.

It is so incredibly difficult for them to endure loneliness. It burrows like a gnawing ghost and can no longer be shaken off.

There is nothing to replace their absence and they are not trying. They are wrong if they believe my God could fill the gap to give them strength and confidence during this time. He does not do it! He keeps them unfilled and helps them to maintain their close connection with the daughter.

The gratitude of the parents for spending time with their daughter turns the pain of memory into a quiet joy and a precious gift. Parents often ask themselves quietly and despondently, will we be able to live again as in previous years? Will our laughter find its way through the common spaces again? Where should we put the pain and how and where should we keep the burden of the pain? Because a soul pain of this kind does not pass and does not subside or does it? No! He holds her and does not let go of her. It penetrates deep into the parents' heart and is inextricably attached to their lives and their souls. It will only pass if they both go to another world.

In the end, it will be suffering, toil and love for her that make time without it essential, that will give it weight and depth. The father remembers the birth of the daughter. At that time, they embedded joy and love into them. Isn't it understandable that life tries to slip away because it was taken from them? It is part of them, their life and their soul. How should they live on without them?

The friends, colleagues and neighbors do not hold back with wellintentioned advice. You have to let go! You can't change it anyway and life goes on and doesn't stop!

Distract yourself! Dive into work. Say it! You have to distance yourself and think about yourself and the future of yourself. You can't bring your daughter back. As if all of this made sense and could replace the grief and pain of the parents.

Perhaps they will admire the mourners one time or another if they are not put down by the heavy burden of grief and despair. You control yourself or sometimes show a smile. They think that with grief everything is over and the everyday life returns. You will get over it. Claim it! That is certainly meant lovingly, but it is terribly unsuspecting.

Do you want to stay where the daughter had to leave her? On the dark boundary between the two worlds? Do you find the courage and the strength to continue living here?

Mourners today find it particularly difficult to cope with the time of suffering. They hear incessantly what terrible and cruel things happen in this world every day. People who are haunted by misfortune and the fear and their fate, who don't let anyone come to rest. How can the mourners react to this?

Forget quickly! Distract! Repress everything and put it away in the most untraceable mental chambers! This is what you expect from those affected.

The friends talk to them about everything, only not about the terrible event, the death of their daughter. Don't touch it! They think.

What helps you? To kill pain and grief in a frenzy? Escape from the house or hide in the infinity of life? No!

Crying with your soul because you are without your daughter and your heart is writhing in cramps, more than any mother or father can judge about the injustice that has hit her, yes! To be infuriated! Screaming even when someone hears or sees it. Quarrel with God who allowed that! Be quiet when you feel that others cannot understand you! Seek rest if you are too tired to talk or if you feel guilty!

One day it may not be so important to cry or scream, but now it is good for them. And now nobody should take it from them.

No use running away! Where should they go? Drowning yourself in alcohol is of no use, waking up is all the more terrible. They don't know if the sun will shine for them again someday. They are in their house protecting the daughter. A house that consisted of them together. Now she is no longer here. The violent death has sent them to another world in which they are still unable to follow.

On a day when the sun is trying to find a small path through the dark, cloudcovered sky, you will see a small rainbow while walking, which makes a colorful effort to show its colorful arch. It invites you to go back and forth like a bridge. Over and over, just for walking.

Your grief is such a hike. Over there where the daughter had to go and back where they were together. All the years of living together. This back and forth is important for them! The memories stay awake for them and bring them back together! The parents' cry for their daughter is like an unfulfilled longing. Your heart suffers from the burden and calls it back! But it doesn't really heal. You have to go your way on earth so that you can follow your daughter. That the way to her leads her closer and that the daughter can find the parents. Or do they want to go to her now and not just when God calls her?

It is difficult for parents not to succumb to this temptation. Grief is like death itself. And is it cowardly if you want to be home where it is? Or do they have to mature mentally first? It would be good for the parents to stay on Earth for a while until the day has light and sun again.

Because here should arise what is seen in their life as meaning and value and everything has a goal.

The parents stand close to their daughter's grave and ask:

"Will we see our daughter again?"

Both believe and feel this firmly with their hearts and souls and they will find them!

Author

The time comes when the 65th year of life is within reach, finally one thinks with relief, retired. So far so good! It doesn't take long before the 66th birthday is celebrated with the family and, with increasing impatience, it becomes clear that such a day, with its 24 hours, can be quite long.

Family, grandchildren, lazing around, traveling and occasional botanical experiments in gardening are no longer enough to give the day an interesting face, what to do? You can't get around this question if you don't want to spend the rest of your life on the couch and in front of the TV. Why, I asked myself, rethink the many thoughts and ideas that have accumulated over the course of a lifetime and, if possible, process them in writing. As soon as such thoughts are thought through to the end, the necessary initiative develops. Literature studies are required. If the head thinks without thinking about the body, it is already 66 years old. It was these three years of study that show-ed me that creative writing doesn't have to remain a dark secret if you try to air it. And something else helped me a lot to tackle writing seriously. The spiritual "listen in" to look for conversations with the consciousness and his inner voice.

Many of my friends and readers have been asking me for a long time, how are you doing writing so many books in such a short time? Frankly, I can't even answer this see-mingly simple question myself. I think it is my inner voice that wants to argue with me all the time. And so thet-houghts flow almost automatically into the keyboard of my computer as if directed by a ghost.

Content Description

Animals play an important role in these exciting and thoughtful stories.

Timon, completely stunned that animals can also think and speak, experiences exciting adventures with his crawling ghosts and the bear Billy.

He saves his new girlfriend, the fly Liesa, from starvation.

The bee Susi, together with her friend Liesa and Timon, is fighting for an injured bee that can escape bad men with all its strength.

Together with his girlfriend Liesa and the bear Billy, they release a family of collar bears from the terrible and painful torture of the poachers.